Where's My T·R·U·C·K?

by **Karen Beaumont**

pictures by **David Catrow**

Dial Books for Young Readers
an imprint of Penguin Group (USA) Inc.

"Shhh!" I hear my parents say,
"Tommy's not himself today.
He's lost his T·R·U·C·K!"

My brother says, "Let's climb a tree."
My sister says, "Play house with me."
But all I want to do today
Is find my T·R·U·C·K!

I look behind my closet door.
I dig through every dresser drawer.

I search my brother's pile of junk.
I look in Grandma's smelly trunk.

And underneath the bed . . .

And chair.

Behind the curtain . . .
OOPS! Not there!

I CANNOT FIND IT ANYWHERE!

My brother tosses me a ball.
My sister hands me some dumb doll.
My mom says it will be okay.
My dad just shrugs and walks away.

I WANT MY T·R·U·C·K!

I dump my toy box on the floor.
I look . . .
And look . . .
And look some more.

I've never lost my truck before.

I go outside . . .
Where could it be?
Is it underneath the tree?

In the sandbox?
By the shed?
Maybe in the
flower bed?

I climb
up on
the ladder . . .
Hey!

Is that my T·R·U·C·K?

I look again
but still
no luck.

Did someone
steal my
favorite truck?

I had my
red truck
yesterday.

A toy truck
can't just
drive away!

My brother hands me his green jeep.
My dad says I just need more sleep.
My sister says, "Come on. Let's play!"
My mom just whispers, "What a day."

I WANT MY T·R·U·C·K!

I don't want jeeps or cars or planes,
Or boats or bikes or trikes or trains.
I don't want green or blue or black.
I only want my red truck back.

I look once more out on the lawn.

MY T·R·U·C·K IS GONE!

I loved that truck.
I love it still.
I always, always, always will.

That truck hauled toys
and tools and rocks,
Banana peels and dirty socks,
Great big bones for Bowser . . .

Wait!
What's he doing
by the gate?

Bowser's dug a giant hole.
Something's buried by his bowl.
Something . . . kind of red . . .

Come on, Bowser!

Let's go play!

With all my love to John,
who likes big trucks, fast cars,
and other toys that go vroom!
—KB

To Bob Alexander,
the first artist I ever knew.
—DC

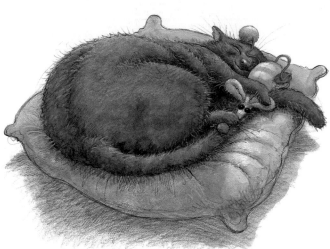

DIAL BOOKS FOR YOUNG READERS
A division of Penguin Young Readers Group
Published by The Penguin Group
Penguin Group (USA) Inc., 375 Hudson Street, New York, NY 10014, U.S.A.
Penguin Group (Canada), 90 Eglinton Avenue East, Suite 700, Toronto, Ontario,
Canada M4P 2Y3 (a division of Pearson Penguin Canada Inc.)
Penguin Books Ltd, 80 Strand, London WC2R 0RL, England
Penguin Ireland, 25 St. Stephen's Green, Dublin 2, Ireland (a division of Penguin Books Ltd)
Penguin Group (Australia), 250 Camberwell Road, Camberwell,
Victoria 3124, Australia (a division of Pearson Australia Group Pty Ltd)
Penguin Books India Pvt Ltd, 11 Community Centre, Panchsheel Park, New Delhi - 110 017, India
Penguin Group (NZ), 67 Apollo Drive, Rosedale, Auckland 0632,
New Zealand (a division of Pearson New Zealand Ltd)
Penguin Books (South Africa) (Pty) Ltd, 24 Sturdee Avenue, Rosebank, Johannesburg 2196, South Africa
Penguin Books Ltd, Registered Offices: 80 Strand, London WC2R 0RL, England

Designed by Lily Malcom
Text set in Slappy
Manufactured in China on acid-free paper

10 9 8 7 6 5 4 3 2 1

ISBN 978-0-8037-3222-3
Special Markets ISBN 978-0-525-42594-6 Not for resale

Library of Congress Cataloging-in-Publication Data Available

The art was created using pencil and watercolor.